Just a Passing Phrase IV

Mary Easty

Collated by Richard Easty

Contents

Annie Says

Annie's nephew is getting a bit cheeky — she hopes it's just a passing phrase.

A Winter Funeral

Auntie Mabel was well over 90 years old. Many of her contemporaries had already *gone before*, and it was no surprise when during a very cold spell last year we had the sad news of the death of one of her childhood friends, Ellen Bell, known to the family as Auntie Nellie, dearly loved by us all, particularly for her sense of humour. Auntie Mabel wanted to go to the funeral in the next town, so I took her, well wrapped-up, in the car. The only other mourners in the echoing church were an elderly couple we had not met before. They introduced themselves as George and Mattie Moss, former neighbours of Ellen's.

After the service our forlorn little group gathered like frozen crows in the churchyard. George told us that Nellie was to be buried in the family grave.

The familiar solemn ceremony over, we stood about uncertainly in the lashing rain, until I offered to drive Mr and Mrs Moss home. It turned out that they lived quite a long way out of town, so I set off along the motorway with my silent passengers. Shaking with the cold myself, I felt quite concerned about them, sad and numb, so I turned into the service station and parked as near as possible to the restaurant. We shuffled from the car through the downpour, our breath caught and blown away by the gusts of wind, into the noisy entrance hall. I found them some seats and set off for the counter with my plastic tray.

As I returned to their table with four steaming mugs, there was a new spirit afoot - animated faces, beaming smiles. To my astonishment Auntie Mabel and the Mosses were waving to the other customers, bowing with Victorian dignity to people passing them. As I joined them, Mrs Moss said, "I never knew Nellie had such a large circle of friends!" and Auntie Mabel waved to a man across the room. "I can see the minister over there! Such a touching service!" "Just what Nellie would have liked!" trilled Mrs Moss. Unfortunately she caught the eye of a plump young man balancing a doughnut on the top of his plateful of pastries. Blushing, he quickly put it back and disappeared amongst the crowd. Mr Moss got up and walked about, introducing himself as "an old friend of Ellen's" to amazed lorry-drivers and embarrassed motor-cyclists in wet leathers.

I rounded them up after some time, and the talk turned to the funeral ceremony. Mr Moss told us that he had been very fortunate in finding Nellie's "Grave Papers", which apparently entitled her to a niche in the family mausoleum. "Did you know her parents?" he asked me, reading the official sheet, "James and Susannah Bell?"

"They were long before my time," I told him, and asked Auntie Mabel if she had known the Bells. "I didn't know Mr Bell," she replied, "but Auntie Bess was a great favourite of mine." "Bess?" I thought, startled. Then Mrs Moss joined in. "We never met any of her brothers," she said.

I was getting worried. Nellie had only had one, called Peter, as I knew very well. Apparently the Grave Papers made reference to several men, none of whom was called Peter. As further revelations followed, I began to realise that perhaps Nellie had gone to her eternal rest in the wrong place. I was glad she had had such a good sense of humour. . .

Auntie Mabel and the Mosses were by now great friends, and continued to talk loudly about the funeral, all at the same time and luckily not listening to each other at all. If they fell silent for a second, they smiled and waved across the room, sometimes calling "Poor Ellen! She would have been so pleased to see you here!" As I shepherded them out at last to take them home, Auntie Mabel paused at the door and addressed the assembled company in a loud voice.

"It has been a lovely day! Thank you all so much for coming!"

Annie Says

Annie admires the way the government is tackling the credit crunch, but she reminded us we're not out of the woodwork yet.

The Girls

When we were on holiday in Hereford, our friend Jonathan took us to visit his sister. "Philippa and John have a glut of fruit this year," he told us, "she would be glad if we took some... and," he added temptingly, "you could meet her Girls." He wouldn't give any more details, but we were intrigued.

It was late summer, the last hot golden days, and Philippa had set out tea in the garden. She was a tall, angular woman about my own age, who seemed to be wearing rather a lot of clothes - several long skirts, layered one on top of another, a thin shirt over a blouse, topped with a lacy jacket, necklaces, ribbons and scarves, and a kerchief over her hair. She looked a splendid, colourful figure, and I looked round hopefully for some little daughters, imagining them with long plaits and starched pinafores over their cotton frocks.

The house was tall too, and like herself covered with layers of different textures: flowing ivy, prickly holly, a final flurry of creamy roses, seed heads of fading clematis. We sat in the warm sunshine and admired the view which spread for miles around us. Everywhere was very quiet. Perhaps the Girls were not home from school yet.

After tea, Philippa asked if we would like to pick some plums and damsons to take home, and handed out deep wicker baskets. Opening a gate at the end of the garden, she led us into her orchard.

The trees were so heavy with fruit that they bent down to the ground, and some of the branches had broken off. We greedily stocked up with far more fruit than we could possibly need, and discussed bottling and freezing and jam-making, knowing perfectly well that we should probably make ourselves so ill with over-eating that we would not be able to indulge in any of these worthy activities.

"Are you going to show us your Girls?" Jonathan said at last, as we rather shame-facedly came to a halt. "Oh yes! but of course!" his sister agreed enthusiastically. We turned towards the house, expecting the children to appear at last, but Philippa opened another gate in the hedge. "Come on!" she called softly. "Come on, Girls!" and in trotted a line of strange-looking lambs - strange because they had unusually-shaped heads, marked boldly in black and white stripes.

"Here are my Girls!" Philippa said proudly. "May I introduce my badger-faced sheep!" Jonathan laughed at our astonishment. They were quite beautiful, and we could see why they were called badger-faced, the markings made them exactly that. Philippa's "Girls" were not kept for meat or wool, but to win prizes in their category at the Shows. She was so successful that the other breeders teased her about having a secret weapon! She teased them in turn by looking mysterious.

Each year, she told us, she named the new lambs in alphabetical order as they were born, and each grew to recognise and answer to her own name. The first Girls had been given Girls' names, the second were flowers, and this year the new babies were the Spice Girls, for obvious reasons! She counted them off, and I can remember most of them - Aniseed, Bergamot, Coriander, Dill, Fennel; there was Ginger, Juniper, Marjoram, Nutmeg, Oregano, Paprika, Saffron and Tarragon, beautiful names for beautiful creatures! One of the little lambs ran directly to me, nuzzling my hands and nosing in my basket. I was absurdly pleased to be chosen in this way and immediately fell in love with her. Philippa introduced me: "This is Nutmeg," and I said, "Hello, Nutmeg, what a pretty name for such a pretty girl."

"She is one of the really good lambs this year," Philippa told us. "I'm taking some of them to the Show at Ross tomorrow, and Nutmeg will certainly be in the team. Next time you see her, she should be wearing a rosette."

When they had been petted, the Girls rushed into the orchard and foraged amongst the trees even more greedily than we had done. I was surprised to see how much they loved the fruit, clambering over each other to gulp down huge quantities. As we watched, we heard a loud crack as a branch snapped off, and the flock raced across, jumping high in the air in their haste to get there first. They fell on the damsons like the plague of locusts in the Biblical fields of corn. Philippa beamed as they champed and guzzled, and assured us it would do them no harm - they were obviously well-used to the fruit, and were still busy when we left, their striped heads buried in the tall grass under the trees.

Next evening we phoned to thank Philippa for our visit, and asked how she had gone on at the Show. The Girls had scored highly, she said, and had won some individual rosettes and a cup for being Best of Breed. What about the damsons? we wondered. Philippa laughed. Pens are not prepared at the shows, she told us, but fencing is available so owners can set up their own corrals for their animals. She had arranged her pen and settled the lambs in, and walked around to assess the competition and see the other breeds. After the judging she had received her prizes and congratulations, then loaded the Girls into the truck. When she went back to remove her fencing she found a crowd standing all round the pen, staring at the ground. Every blade of grass was hidden - covered with plum and damson stones! Her secret weapon, indeed!

Brief Encounter

I had a brief but welcome encounter a few years ago. I had arranged to stay overnight with some friends, breaking my journey south. They live in a very quiet spot, outside a village called Bellford, and their house is in a tiny hamlet with a lovely name, it's called World's End.

I made good time until I turned off the main road in Wiltshire and looked for the sign to Bellford. There it was at last, and I shot off onto the narrow road, only to come very quickly on a sign blocking my route, "Road closed, flooding." I hit the brakes, as the best novels say, and pulled up. What could I do now? I would remember the way to Word's End down this road and subsequent narrow lanes, another 10 miles at least, but if I couldn't get through I had no idea which way to go. These roads have steep banks and there were no landmarks to be seen.

I consulted my useless maps and was beginning to think I might have to get out my useless mobile phone... actually the maps and phone would be useful to anybody else, I'm the useless component there... when bright lights and loud brakes announced the arrival of another car, like me caught up in the problem. This was a big expensive car and the driver got out and slammed his door, very annoyed about this nuisance.

"Seems we can't get through" he called. Yes, I thought, I had noticed that too. "I'll just have a look" and he walked forward a little. I waited for a splash, but he returned quite quickly. "The bridge is down," he said, "we'll have to go round the other way." I peered at him through the window. "Can you give me any directions?" I asked hopefully. "Where are you making for?" he asked. "I'm going to the ends of the earth" I said. "Do you know how to get there?"To my astonishment he started to laugh. "The ends of the earth!" he repeated, "well, it looks as though it can't be far."

He gave me some directions, go back to the main road, turn right turn left cross over and so on but soon realised I had given up. Now he could see I was a rather worried elderly lady he stopped laughing. "I know the back roads" he said, "I fish round here. I'll lead the way and you can follow me...to the ends of the earth".

Of course by then I realised why he had laughed, but was grateful for the help. He drove ahead constantly looking back to make sure we hadn't got separated. In my time I've done a lot of following the car in front and it isn't easy, if the leader suddenly speeds up someone often passes and fills the gap, so I kept my full attention on the Jag. After a long winding 12 or so miles I began to recognise familiar landmarks, and we got to Bellford and the final lane. My rescuer still led the way, and eventually I saw the sign for World's End and the lights of my friends' house.

They hurried out to the car to welcome me, and when they saw my rescuer and we explained what had happened, they shook his hand and thanked him. "That was good of you, Jeremy", they said. "Oh, I was pleased to help," he replied.

In the lamplight I suddenly recognised him!

When I see him on TV and hear people talking about him, I say mysteriously "I once followed that man to the ends of the earth".

Seed of Doubt

I can still remember the day when Joan Taylor sowed the seed! I know where we all were, huddled around the smoky, smelly, solid-fuel stove which was intended to warm the pre-fabricated huts the first form used for lessons, bombs having destroyed the old buildings. As we swung on the fireguards, Joan rushed in, late, wet and excited. "Angela Galloway's mother is a spy!" she gasped.

Our chatter stopped and we stared at her. I noticed that some girls' mouths actually did drop open, like ham actors' when the stage directions read "shock." "How do you know?" "What do you mean?" we screeched when we re-gathered our wits.

Joan was trying to look caring and sympathetic, judge-mental and patriotic, mysterious but knowing, all at the same time. Difficult! Her face was red and her eyes shining as she filled us in.

Angela Galloway had joined our class late in the term, and none of us knew much about her. We had heard that her mother was "a foreigner" as the term was then, a nurse who worked at the Nursing Home where she and Angela lived.

Joan's information was sparse but absolutely astounding. Joan's Dad, on duty as an air-raid warden, had seen Angela and her mother picked up by uniformed men and taken away in a military car, looking very upset. "My Dad says that Mrs Galloway is a German," said Joan, her voice loaded with meaning.

We stared. A German spy in our own neighbourhood! Some of the girls, whose fathers were in the forces, looked very worried. Had they said anything in Angela's hearing that could have put their relations in danger? "Careless talk costs lives" as we all knew.

The seed Joan had planted had fallen on fertile ground, and took root immediately. By home time, every girl in the school had picked it up, and great tubers spread rapidly when they got home and told their families. Budding detectives remembered remarks Angela had made in class — wishing we learnt German, not French, for example, and comments in Geography lessons about European rivers. Suddenly it seemed strange that Angela had not accepted invitations to call for anyone on the way to school, or invited anyone to her house, admittedly difficult as she lived over the Home, but still, what was there to hide from our eyes? And as someone mentioned, she had never spoken of her father.

In the weeks that followed, rumours spread like weeds, and all this stemmed from the one fact we knew from the beginning, that Angela and her mother had been driven off in a staff car by some soldiers. There were little off-shoots of gossip — mothers remembered Mrs Galloway hurrying furtively past them in the shops, somebody's dad home on leave thought he had heard the name Galloway mentioned somewhere. Many girls were glad that Angela had not been to their house to spy — others sorry not to have had the chance to spy on hers. We agreed that there had always been something odd about the Galloways.

Then on the last day of term, the head called a special Assembly. We stood in rows in our flowery cotton frocks, our faces warm in the early spring sunshine. The closing service followed the usual traditions. Then: "Before we break up for Easter," she said, "I have an extra announcement to make."

A little ripple of movement, like the lightest breeze in a

garden, moved amongst us. The first year blossomed smugly — this would specially concern us!

"Many of you will know," she said, "that one of our juniors, Angela Galloway, has not been at school for a week or two. Some of you may have met Angela's mother, who comes from Germany. Mrs Galloway was the matron of a very prestigious hospital in Cologne, but as war approached she was warned to leave the country because her husband was an English soldier. After great hardships, Mrs Galloway and Angela managed to escape and were brought to live in our town. Angela's father continued to serve in the British army, but sadly has just lost his life, bravely defending his men at Dunkirk. Colonel Galloway has been posthumously awarded the George Medal in recognition of his courage, and Angela and her mother were taken to London to receive this honour on his behalf from the King. Angela will not be returning to school after the holiday — her mother has accepted the post of Matron at a military hospital in the South." "I am aware," she added, "that there has been quite a lot of unnecessary and uninformed gossip..."

The Head glanced down at us from the platform. We were all wriggling about with embarrassment, cut down by her withering look, our heads drooping. For a moment her face softened. "I am sure, first years," she said, "you would like a few minutes in your form room before you break up for the holiday. Perhaps you might like to compose a note for Angela." And she motioned to our form teacher to lead the way.

Life in a Goldfish Bowl

7-year-old Matthew went to stay with his grandparents. When his mother phoned to see how the visit was going, he was very positive. "It's great!" he told her. "Grandpa's taking me to the fair tomorrow!" His brother Peter was listening too. "He never used to take me out like that!" Peter complained. "Nor me!" said their father, "doesn't sound like my Dad!"

When they phoned the next day, there was even more rejoicing. "I won a goldfish!" was the boast, and Peter got even more annoyed. "I never had a goldfish" he moaned. Matthew's grandmother was surprised too. The entertainment was usually left to her when the boys came. Grandpa was being very kind. He'd even bought a big round bowl for Matthew's fish. "I'm going to call him Chips," Matthew told them.

When his father came to take him home in the car that evening, Matthew held the bowl, and Chips in his plastic bag, carefully on his knee. The bowl was set in the middle of the table, and everyone came in to admire the goldfish as he swam slowly round and round. "How kind of Grandpa," everyone agreed.

After a bit, Matthew was worried: "Shouldn't we put something in the bowl so Chips can sit down and have a rest?" "I don't think goldfishes sit down very much," his father replied."

"But he's swimming such a long way," said Matthew. "I wonder how many lengths he's done already?" "He can't do lengths in that!" Peter was dismissive. "It would be rounds." Matthew was still worried. "The bowl's round all the way," Matthew complained, "he wouldn't know where he'd started."

"Is he doing breast stroke?" Peter teased him. Matthew

took it seriously, and stared at Chips." "Fishes don't have breasts," he decided, so Peter said "what about crawl?" and as Matthew started to get cross his father joined in quickly, before Peter could say "what about back stroke?" which could have caused an unfortunate argument, saying "This lovely bowl that Grandpa bought for you is Chips' new world."

There was a pause, as everyone looked at him. He realised he had sounded rather pompous, and made it worse by saying "a world of air and water and glass. . ." as his wife turned away to hide a smile. "Every world has its limitations," he added, and was glad when Matthew broke in "Doesn't he look funny when he goes round corners?"

Peter was just saying "there aren't any corners" when his father said "it's because of the glass, of course, reflections and perspective," and added sharply "get down at once" as Matthew climbed onto a chair to look more closely.

"I wonder what it's like to live in a glass room" was Matthew's next remark. "Awful!" said Peter immediately, "it would be awful in school! They would see if you looked at somebody else's answers." " They would know if you were eating sweets" said Matthew, "or looked at your mobile phone" said Peter, "scratched your bottom!" contributed Matthew "Yes, alright" their mother said quickly, to put a stop to this. She was just going to suggest dinner, realising Chips' world of air and water and glass would have to be moved, when Matthew said "Grandpa has a glass room!" Everyone looked at him. Now what was he thinking about?

"I know!" said Peter after a second. "His greenhouse. That's a glass room".

"But when Grandpa's in there people can't see him, it's right down the garden," said his father. "I can!" said Matthew. "I can see him from my bedroom window when I stay with them. I watched him the other day, smoking a cigarette. He told me he would take me to the fair if I didn't tell anyone, so I didn't."

Annie Says

Annie's planning for the summer. She's considering a Sago holiday.

Door Stepping

From my first day at school at the age of five to the last day many years later, my morning started at the front door of my great friend Margaret. I would reach up to the knocker, and turn to smile at my mother waiting at the top of the road. Usually, Margaret's mother would open the door and ask me in, with a big hug, and my mother could go home, and I would sit in their front room, which always smelt of apples. Sometimes I had to jump back, as Margaret flew out, satchel swinging dangerously, and we raced up the road on the last minute. After a few weeks I could find my way on my own, and this set the pattern.

Their door was just like all the others in the road, except for the number, of course, shiny brown with a little window above my head. But as I grew taller and less oblivious of my surroundings, one day I spotted a square metal notice above the key-hole. It read NO HAWKERS CIRCULARS. I read the notice every morning and forgot about it immediately, as we had so much to chatter about. In any case, it seemed rude to mention it, and anyway I wasn't sure I was reading it correctly, but I did begin to wonder what it meant and why it was there.

One evening I asked my father what circular meant. "Well, you know the roundabout outside the Library?" he replied from behind the Daily Dispatch. "Circular means that shape. Round." I wasn't convinced, but you didn't argue with my father. Another day I asked my mother "What's a Hawker?" She was busy getting the tea ready, but she had loved history when she was at school. "I think it's a huntsman on a horse, going after rabbits, with a huge bird on his arm." She continued to add details about catching prey, but I had started thinking

15

"No Hawkers Circulars"... Why did Margaret's mother not have any? I wondered, and why did she have a notice on her door to say so? We didn't have any either but we didn't bother telling everybody.

I read the notice again every morning, and in the end I wrote it down before I knocked on the door, and showed it to my parents that evening. They laughed for ages, and my mother said "Oh, it's like Mr. Hartley." And they were laughing so much I still didn't understand.

At that time, late thirties, early forties, the War was on, and a major feature of that for us was the blackout. Special thick curtains covering all the windows to prevent any chink of light bringing down the Warden's wrath, no streetlamps, utter blackness outside. In the summer we could play out until the sun went down, but autumn and winter streets were dangerous. We came home from school, had our tea, did our homework, and then entertained ourselves, reading, playing games, sometimes listening to the wireless (but that was really for the grownups) crayoning and writing—and some little girls could sew, knit, even crochet. Some little girls, but not me. I was absolutely hopeless at anything to do with hands — still am — but I LOVED collecting the Kit. And this is where Mr. Hartley came in, for he was our Hawker Circular.

I remember every detail of him, for we loved him dearly. My memories of him are all connected with the blackout. Perhaps he did come in the summer,but we must have been out playing. He came on Thursdays at six o'clock, and we would rush to the door. The night would be dark, often wet, sometimes snowy, and I remember mist and even fog around his outline. We heard his cough as he waited on the step. He wore a hat and a long overcoat, had a pale face, glasses, his thin hair straight and grey combed back under the trilby. He had a pronounced stoop, and no wonder when you tried to lift his suitcase, hard to believe he managed to carry it from door to door.

Our house, built in the twenties, had quite a wide hall. My mother kept a hard wooden chair near the door, next to a piece of furniture called a dinner-wagon, a sort of wooden trolley with the phone on top and a shelf underneath.

Mr. Hartley was always invited in, the same conversation each week like a play. "Will you come in for a few minutes, Mr. Hartley?" "Thankyou very much, if it's not inconvenient." "Not at all. Can I offer you a cup of tea?" "Oh, that would be most welcome." He would put his hat on the dinner-wagon and heave his heavy case over the threshold, a brass frame which we had to polish when we did our Saturday jobs, and we always hoped he wouldn't scratch it. We would fetch him tea and leave cake on the dinner-wagon, and were sent away whilst he consumed it. If my father was home from work, he would come and have an awkward chat with him, awkward because Mr. H. was often wearing one of my father's jerseys or twiddling his former hat.

After a time, we would be called into the hall and Mr. Hartley would be invited to open his case-just "to see if we need anything" my mother would say. She might buy pegs or a floor cloth or hairpins. We always needed something. Skeins of wools in brilliant colours, embroidery silks, pieces of lace or ribbon. We knew we could only afford one purchase each, and only had a little pocket money and might have to borrow from each other. When Mr. Hartley left, we could hear the coughing again as he assumed his rounds.

As we grew up we hardly noticed when he stopped coming. Maybe the cough caught up with him. By then perhaps the blackouts were over. Not many Mr. Hartleys about today! The few who do come are not often the ones you would want (or dare) to invite over the doorstep. Their cases are full of badly-made things at inordinate prices, and there is always the worry that they are really "casing the joint." Happy memories though of a lovely gentle man... and still a secret smug smile that his route didn't take him to Margaret's road... which is probably the reason, I suppose, why Margaret's mother didn't have a Hawker Circular.

Annie Says

Everybody makes mistakes, says Annie. Even the worst of us have our flaws.

Charity Begins at Home

Laura opened her wardrobe. This was to be the day of reckoning. She unloaded all the hangers and riffled through her blouses. All clean, ironed and still as they were when she put them away last summer. Or was it the summer before? The lacy ones could go, too thin. The pink one that had been mended so carefully that it didn't show, nobody could possibly tell, except her, but, never mind, keep that, an old favourite. All the T shirts were too tight even last year, add them to the pile. Why had she bought that yellow thing? Never put it on, never would. Now for the frocks. Too short, all three of them. She turned her attention to the coats. Had she ever worn that dreadful purple thing? Smoothing them out and folding them she carefully filled the bags.

Now for the other rooms. She had already put out some ashtrays, not in use any more since her sons had left home, and a couple of dishes that had been her mother's. Two or three bowls they had grown bulbs in, a brass windmill and a pretty cup and saucer. A few other ornaments were slipped into the bag and she closed it quickly and went downstairs.

As she ate her boiled egg she reminded herself that she was pleased to have made a bit of room upstairs. They were nice things and she didn't look at them again in case she wanted them back, like a child who reluctantly gives away a present she wants for herself. These things have played a part in my life, she thought, that's what I'm giving away.

So, after lunch, before she could change her mind, she set out, feeling quite proud that she was giving things to someone who would be glad of them. This is what charity means, she thought.

Then as she went into the shop she suddenly had horrid doubts. What if the woman said "we don't want rubbish like this, you should be ashamed. Take it back," rejecting her and her life and her possessions? People would stare and judge.

The shop was warm and bright, the wares set out nicely, good things that looked almost new but attractively old. The woman took the bag without a glance inside, and smiled and thanked her, and handed it to a girl who took it through a door to a room that Laura could see was stacked with boxes and huge bags waiting to be sorted. Laura turned away and left quickly, suddenly a bit tearful, pushing her way past other women bringing their contributions. She walked home quickly, hoping that when the girl came to sort her bags she wouldn't sniff or laugh, but arrange them on display with other pretty things, so they would be chosen to be part of other people's life. . . and not be put in the box outside with HELP YOURSELF written in red letters of shame.

Around the Corner

"You never know what's round the corner" mothers used to say. I thought I knew what they meant, something on the lines of "one door closes, another opens," clouds with silver lining... Of course, at that time I didn't know June Connolly. Nowadays, I do know what's round the corner, and it's usually June.

June's house is quite close to mine, and when I go out I glance suspiciously to the left as I reach my gate. Generally, the coast is clear, but as I emerge I'll hear the neighbourly cry "hello, Stranger! How are you?" and the click of the little shoes as June hurries up. I see the smiling little lips, and above them the glittering little eyes, and behind those I can see the busy little brain processing what she is seeing. "She's lost a lot of weight" June is thinking, or "goodness, how fat she's getting," She thinks "why does she wear green, it doesn't suit her" or "she used to wear that coat when she was pushing the pram!" and all the time I can see that she is sorry for me. The shining day fades so I change the subject as she falls into step with me. "How are you?" she says. "Fine!" I say, but I see the wry smile. "How brave!" her expression tells me, to my rage. "How are you?" I retaliate, as the strength seeps from my legs...

"I'm fine,"she'll say. And then "not like poor Alison." Alison is her next door neighbour. "That new baby screams all night! Nobody gets any sleep! I've told her she should feed it every time it cries but she can't seem to get it right."

"Isn't it sad about Mr Birch?" I stare at her in surprise. "I thought he was out of hospital" I say, but "Oh, yes, but he can't do anything for himself, with that arm in a sling. People forget about that. I go round when I can..." and her voice will trail off as she contemplates her generosity.

There's a "poor dog" that barks all day, June thinks the owners don't love it. She talks to it over the fence so it won't be lonely. Some people in the road don't know how to bring up their children, always hungry so June gives them little treats.

June Connolly feels sympathy for everybody in our area, everybody in the world. She is sorry for Mr Brown and Mr Cameron and that nice young (too young) Mr Whatever his name is, one or two of them are bound to lose the election.

And as she empathises and feels their pain, the clouds are closing in over our heads and I'm desperately hoping to be rescued. Sometimes a bus approaches and I get on, regardless of its destination. Sometimes I dive into a shop or remember something I should have brought with me and turn back.

The problem I have is that too often I do know what is round the corner, and too often it turns out to be the caring and kindly June Connolly.

Annie Says

Annie is delighted! Her son has just bought her the latest short-circuit TV!

Welcome

One evening last week I was peeling potatoes when I heard the doorbell ring. On the doorstep was a young woman that I felt I had seen before but couldn't quite recognise. She seemed to know me and just said "Hello, Mary!" and walked past me into the hall, smiling. "It's lovely to see you," she said, "I have always wanted to come." Somehow I too felt really pleased, and all I did was to step back and invite her into the kitchen. "Hope you don't mind, I'm just..." but she interrupted "Oh no, that's all right, I expected you would be busy. Is everybody at home at present?"

I explained who would and who wouldn't be in for the evening meal and wondered whether she should be invited to stay, but held back. Then "Tell me about them all whilst you are cooking" and she settled on a chair as we talked. As I put the food into dishes and the dishes into the oven, set the cooker from six till seven o'clock and set the table, I told her about the family, and she would add little questions like "how old is he?" and "where is she now" and I still felt quite comfortable as we discussed children and cousins and nieces and she knew all the names.

When I had finished I said "Will you come and sit down on a more comfortable chair?" but she said "I wonder if we could go into the garden? I would really like to see it." There were some old wicker chairs under the holly tree, so I made more cups of tea and we went outside. She obviously loved flowers, specially the roses, which were at their best just then.

All the time, I knew absolutely that I had seen her before. Her face was familiar, and that word lodged in my mind, familiar, she must be a relative. I had seen those eyes, heard that voice. She was the same shape as I am, as was my mother and my aunt, and my daughter is the same. There were other similarities but it was the way she spoke that made me think I must have met her before. I couldn't work out how old she was, perhaps in her late thirties or early forties, but I couldn't place her in the close family and it didn't seem to matter.

It was beginning to get cooler as we chatted, as relaxed as if we met every day. I thought about suggesting we went in, but as if reading my thoughts she stood up and thanked me for my welcome. I suddenly realised that I still didn't know who she was. When she said "Mary, I have always wanted to visit you" I could not bear to miss the chance and said as calmly as I could " I am so pleased you came" and then" I'm so sorry, you remember my name but I've stupidly not been able to remember yours." She turned and looked at me, smiling. "I'm Jennie." That didn't help, as she could see. "I'm the Jane in my generation, Jennie because there have always been so many Janes, your own daughter is Margaret Jane. You are the Mary in your generation," she said, "as your mother was, and your niece is. There's always been a Mary and a Jane, as far back as any one can tell".

We were at the front gate now. I was still confused and couldn't let her go yet. "But which Jane are you?" I prompted. She turned, and looked at me, almost to confront me. "I'm your mother's mother" she said. "But you are so young!" I couldn't help bursting out. "We don't all live to grow old," was the sad reply, and my eyes filled with tears as she walked away out of my sight.

In my kitchen I leaned against the sink and looked into the garden. I found myself staring at the white rose tree, which I brought back from my grandfather's garden when he died, in

1966, aged 98. Would Jennie have known about that? He had planted it in her memory after her death, when her children were very small.

Suddenly, I remembered the dinner I was cooking. Was it burnt? Then I saw the timer. Still set to cook till 7. Just starting off.

Annie Says

Annie saw a photograph of that man who escaped from the Police. He won't get far, she thinks, he's still in cuff-links.

Incident on the 14th floor

Some years ago, when volunteers were appreciated, not examined and rebuffed, Roz volunteered to deliver meals on wheels to the high rise flats in Nottingham. She was the stand-in, when anyone called in sick, Roz took on the work.

One day she was sent to the Robin Hood Tower to take a hot dinner to Elsie Smith, on the 14th floor. Carrying two steaming parcels, she stepped warily into the smelly, creaky, unreliable lift, frightened all the time as it juddered up the shaft in case anyone should climb in and eat Elsie's dinner. As it lurched to a stop, she hurried out and screwing up her face in the dim hallway found Elsie's door, arranging herself in the view of the TV monitor. She could feel the shrewd appraising eyes inspecting her, and held up the parcels to prove her identity. The door opened and she went in.

A large, jolly woman welcomed her like an old friend from her chair by the electric fire. This was a woman obviously cherished by her family. A framed picture on the wall behind her announced "Top Gran" and an embroidered tray cloth read "our Mam". Bouquets of plastic daffodils and roses shone on the window sill, and the table by the chair held a dish of bananas and oranges and a bowl of nuts. "That looks a comfy chair," Roz said. Elsie beamed and demonstrated its best points; at the lightest touch of a button the back could rise and fall, and another button lifted the seat and almost ejected her on to the carpet.

After a few bits of conversation, Roz laid the parcels down and turned to go. Elsie pointed to the fruit. "Will you have some?" she offered. Roz thanked her and refused politely. "Those are meant for you" she said. But Elsie persisted, "Well, at least have some nuts", and as Roz didn't like to refuse again she took a handful and rushed off.

The next day was just the same, Elsie full of comments and news, and as Roz was leaving the nuts were offered again. This time, Elsie had put some into an envelope specially for her.

On the 3rd day, Roz noticed the bowl was still almost over-flowing. When Elsie held it out to her, Roz said "You always seem to have a lot of nuts! Are you very fond of them?" "Oh, no," said Elsie, "I never eat them myself, I don't like them at all." "Why do you buy them, then?" Roz asked. "My son brings them", Elsie explained, "He does my shopping for me every week." "Well, why don't you tell him you don't like them?" "Oh, I couldn't do that!" Elsie was very determined. "I couldn't hurt his feelings. And anyway, I love the chocolate round them."

Annie Says

Annie's bought some new furniture for her bedroom, a dressing-table and a toyboy. She'll have to move the wardrobe, but it won't be heavy, it's on rafters.

www.ingramcontent.com/pod-product-compliance
Lightning Source LLC
Chambersburg PA
CBHW071228130626
46555CB00004B/1900